Mrs. Jafee Is Daffy!

Mrs. Jafee Is Daffy!

Dan Gutman

Pictures by Jim Paillot

HARPER
An Imprint of HarperCollinsPublishers

To Emma

Mrs. Jafee Is Daffy!

Text copyright © 2009 by Dan Gutman

Illustrations copyright © 2009 by Jim Paillot

Library of Congress Cataloging-in-Publication Data

Gutman, Dan.

    Mrs. Jafee is daffy! / Dan Gutman ; pictures by Jim Paillot. — 1st ed.

       p.   cm. — (My weird school daze ; #6)

    Summary: When the new vice principal is put in charge of Ella Mentry School for a few days, she tries out some very unusual ideas about how students learn.

    ISBN 978-0-06-155413-1 (lib. bdg.) — ISBN 978-0-06-155411-7 (pbk.)

    [1. Schools—Fiction.   2. School principals—Fiction.   3. Humorous stories.]   I. Paillot, Jim, ill.   II. Title.

PZ7.G9846Msj 2009   2009014568

[Fic]—dc22   CIP

                                                                AC

Typography by Joel Tippie

09 10 11 12 13   LP/RRDB   10 9 8 7 6 5 4 3 2 1

❖

First Edition

Contents

The End of Mr. Klutz?

My name is A.J. and I hate school.*

I would rather go shopping for clothes with my mom than go to school. I would rather watch a ballet than go to school. I would rather eat a squirrel that got hit by

---

* Okay, the first sentence is done. Enough reading for the day. You can go play video games now.

a car and was lying in the middle of the road for a week than go to school.

Well, maybe not that last one.

It was Monday, the worst day of the week. Everybody had to go to the all-purpose room, which is a room we use for all purposes, so it has the perfect name.

The whole school was gabbing when our principal, Mr. Klutz, got up on the stage. He was holding a suitcase. Mr. Klutz has no hair at all. I mean *none*. Not even a little on the sides, like my grandpa.

"I have an important announcement to make," said Mr. Klutz.

"Quiet!" said Michael, who never ties his shoes. "Mr. Klutz is gonna make an important announcement!"

"Shhhhh!" said Ryan, who will eat anything. "Mr. Klutz is gonna make an important announcement!"

"Stop talking!" said Neil, who we call the nude kid even though he wears clothes. "Mr. Klutz is gonna make an important announcement!"

We were all buzzing so much about Mr. Klutz's announcement that he couldn't make the announcement that he was trying to announce.

The teachers held up peace signs with their fingers, which means "shut up." But nobody shut up.

Mr. Klutz reached into his pocket and pulled out one of those air horn cans that people bring to football games.

BEEEEEEEEEEEEEEEEEEEEEEEEEEEP!

We all covered our ears and stopped talking.

"Boys and girls, I want to let you know that I have to go to the airport, because I'm leaving—"

WHAT?!

"Mr. Klutz is leaving!" one of the second graders yelled.

Everybody started freaking out, screaming, crying, and falling out of their seats. You should have been there!

"Mr. Klutz isn't going to be our principal anymore!" wailed Andrea Young, this annoying girl in my class with curly brown hair. "He must have been fired!"

4

"We've got to *do* something!" shouted Andrea's crybaby friend, Emily. Then she went running out of the all-purpose room.

Even the teachers were sobbing and blowing their noses into tissues. Well, they blew the *snot* from their noses into the tissues, not the noses

themselves. If they blew their noses into the tissues, their noses would fall off; and it would be weird to walk around without a nose.

"Don't leave us!" wailed Ms. Hannah, the art teacher. She jumped onstage and was hanging on to Mr. Klutz's leg.

"What will we do without you?" moaned Miss Lazar, the custodian.

Mr. Klutz held up the air horn can again.

BEEEEEEEEEEEEEEEEEEEEEEEEEEEP!

Everybody stopped yelling and crying.

"As I was saying," Mr. Klutz said, "I'm leaving . . . for four days."

Oh. That's different.

A New National Holiday

We were all glad that Mr. Klutz wasn't leaving for good, because he's the best principal in the history of the world. One time I got sent to his office for bad behavior and he gave me a candy bar. It was the greatest moment of my life.

After Mr. Klutz's big announcement, we

went back to class with our teacher, Mr. Granite, who is from another planet.

"G'day, mates!" said Mr. Granite. "This week we're going to learn about the Civil War. It was called the War between the States because the Northern states and the Southern states fought each other."

What?! That makes no sense at all.

"If you're gonna have a war," Michael said, "you should fight somebody *else*."

"Yeah," I said. "Having a war with yourself is like punching yourself in the nose."

"Maybe we ran out of other countries to fight," said Ryan, "so we had to fight ourselves."

"Boys are dumbheads," said Andrea, rolling her eyes.

I was going to say "So is your face" to Andrea, but you'll never believe in a million hundred years who walked into the door at that moment.

Nobody, because if you walked into a door it would hurt. But you'll never believe who walked into the door*way*.

It was Mrs. Jafee, the vice principal!

"To what do we owe the pleasure of your company, Mrs. Jafee?" asked Mr. Granite.

(That's grown-up talk for "What are *you* doing here?")

"Howdy, guys and gals!" said Mrs. Jafee. "I'm still new at Ella Mentry School, so I wanted to introduce myself to each class personally. With Mr. Klutz away for four days, I say it's a good chance for us to get to know each other better, by golly."

"Does anybody know what the word 'vice' means in 'vice principal'?" asked Mr. Granite.

A bunch of hands shot in the air. Mr. Granite called on Michael.

"Vice means 'not good enough,'" Michael said. "Like, the vice president isn't good enough to be president."

"Uh, not exactly," said Mrs. Jafee.

I got called on next.

"My dad uses a vice in his workshop to hold stuff," I said. "I took one of my sister's dolls and crushed it in the vice. That was cool."

"Uh, not that kind of vice, A.J.," said Mr. Granite.

Andrea was waving her hands around like somebody who was stranded on a desert island trying to signal a plane. She is so annoying. Andrea keeps a dictionary on her desk so she can look up words and show everybody how smart she is.

"A vice is a bad habit, like smoking, drinking, or gambling," she said.

"Yes, but that's not it either," said Mr. Granite.

Ha! For the first time in her life, Andrea got something wrong! It should be a national holiday. They could call it Dumbhead Andrea Day. We should get that day off from school every year. Nah-nah-nah boo-boo on Andrea! In her face!

"Vice means 'instead of' or 'in the place of,'" Mrs. Jafee told us. "I'm going to be responsible while Mr. Klutz is away. Do you know what it means to be responsible?"

"That means you mess up a lot," I said.

"Any time something goes wrong at my house, my mom says I'm responsible."

Everybody laughed even though I didn't say anything funny.

"You haven't been vice principal for very long, Mrs. Jafee," said Mr. Granite. "Are you sure you have enough experience to be principal?"

"You betcha!" Mrs. Jafee said. "When I sit at my desk, I can see Mr. Klutz's office."

I didn't see what that had to do with anything.

"Where did Mr. Klutz go?" asked Emily.

"He is on his way to Principal Camp," Mrs. Jafee told us. "He's going to learn how to be a better principal."

"But Mr. Klutz is already a great

principal," said Neil the nude kid.

"He'll be even better when he gets back," Mrs. Jafee said.

"Principal Camp sounds like fun," said Emily.

"What if something terrible happens to Mr. Klutz at Principal Camp?" I asked.

"Like what, A.J.?" said Mr. Granite.

"Well, what if his canoe tips over and he drowns in the lake?" I asked.

"They don't have canoes and lakes at Principal Camp, Arlo!" Andrea said, rolling her eyes. She calls me by my real name because she knows I don't like it.

"They do too."

"Do not."

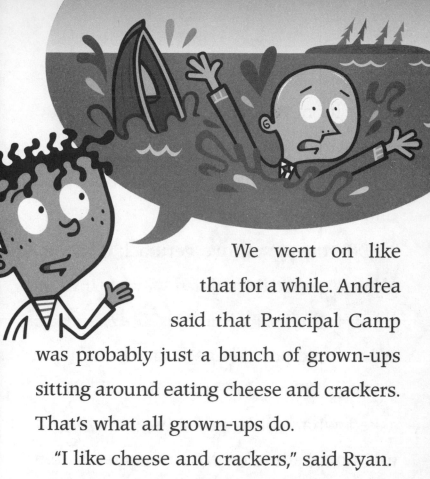

We went on like that for a while. Andrea said that Principal Camp was probably just a bunch of grown-ups sitting around eating cheese and crackers. That's what all grown-ups do.

"I like cheese and crackers," said Ryan.

"What kind of cheese will they have?" asked Michael. "I like monster cheese."

"It's not monster cheese, dumbhead," said Andrea. "It's Muenster cheese."

"Oh, snap!" said Ryan.

"My mom told me there used to be a TV show called *The Munsters*," said Neil.

Mr. Granite made the shut-up peace sign with his fingers.

"Okeydokey, can we get back on topic, please?" asked Mrs. Jafee. "Everything is going to be fine while Mr. Klutz is away. What could possibly go wrong?"

I remember the last time somebody asked what could possibly go wrong. It was our graduation from second grade. I threw my cap in the air and it knocked over the eternal flame and set Emily on fire and Emily freaked out and knocked over the graduation cake and Neil the nude kid almost got trampled by a goat that escaped from the petting zoo and the fire department came and sprayed water on everybody and Andrea's mom and Ryan's mom started wrestling each other and my teacher Miss Daisy fainted and we thought the school security guard was kissing her even though he was just giving her mouth-to-mouth resuscitation and then we found out that Miss Daisy fainted because she was pregnant.

You should have been there!

But I'm sure nothing like that could *possibly* happen this time.

Nice and Calm

When I came into the school on Tuesday morning, I saw the strangest thing in the history of the world: four grown-ups sitting in chairs playing violins!* And they were all dressed up in black suits and dresses! Mrs. Jafee was watching them.

---

* Well, the chairs weren't playing the violins. The people were. If a chair played a violin, it would be weird.

"What's going on?" I asked.

"Mr. Klutz told me he wants everything to be nice and calm while he's away," said Mrs. Jafee. "So I hired a string quartet. Studies show that children can relax and learn better when they listen to soothing music."

"I think we would learn better if we ate lots of ice cream, cookies, cake, and candy," I said.

"Hmmmmm," said Mrs. Jafee.

Grown-ups always say "Hmmmmm" when they're thinking. Nobody knows why.

That's when Little Miss Brownnoser waltzed into the hallway.

"Oh, I just *love* classical music," Andrea

announced (as if anybody asked her). "That's Violin Concerto number 5, by Mozart. I learned about it in the music appreciation class I take after school."

Andrea takes classes in *everything* after school. If they gave a class in picking lint out of your belly button, Andrea would take that class so she could get better at it. Why can't a truck full of violins fall on her head?

The hall was filling up with kids and teachers listening to the boring music.

"Man, that's the fattest violin in the history of the world," I said. "That lady can't even hold it up."

"It's a *cello*, dumbhead!" Andrea said, rolling her eyes.

"Oh, snap!" said Ryan.

"Well, it looks like a violin that needs to go on a diet, if you ask me," I said.

Everybody clapped after the boring

song was over. Then the musicians started playing some other boring song.

"Can you feel the tension *oozing* out of your pores?" Mrs. Jafee said, taking a deep breath. "I learned in graduate school that listening to classical music increases the flow of blood to your brain."

"Ugh, disgusting!" I said. "I don't want blood flowing to my brain."

"Arlo," Andrea said, "if blood didn't flow to your brain, you would die."

I was going to say something mean to Andrea, but I realized that Mrs. Jafee had just said the most amazing thing in the history of the world.

"Wait a minute," I said to her. "Did you just say you went to *graduate school*?"

"You betcha!" she said. "After I finished college, I went to graduate school so I could learn more."

I slapped my forehead. Was she out of her mind? Why would anybody want to go to school after they graduated from school? What is Mrs. Jafee's problem?

"After I graduate," I told her, "I'm not going anywhere *near* a school."

"Well, I spent four years in graduate school studying how children learn," Mrs. Jafee told me. "I'm looking forward to trying some of those new and exciting ideas right here at Ella Mentry School this week. We're going to think outside the box."

Huh? Why would anyone be thinking

in a box to begin with? If I was in a box, I know what I would be thinking about: how to get out of that dumb box! Mrs. Jafee was weird. If she was really a learning expert, she would have learned that after you graduate, you don't have to go to school anymore.

"The music is *soooooooo* beautiful!" Andrea said. "Don't you think so, Arlo?"

"Yeah, just the opposite of your face," I said.

I wanted to say "So is your face." But that would have meant that Andrea is beautiful. And if the guys ever heard me say that, they would say I was in love with her.

So don't ever say "So is your face" after somebody says a word like "nice" or "pretty" or "beautiful." That's the first rule of being a kid.

The New Fizz Ed Teacher

The bell rang, and everybody rushed to their classrooms. We pledged the allegiance with Mr. Granite. Then our computer teacher, Mrs. Yonkers, came into the classroom.

"I have bad news," Mrs. Yonkers told us. "There's no computer class this week."

"Why not?" asked Emily. "I *love* computer class!"

She looked as if she was gonna cry, like always.

"As you know, this is Civil War Week," Mrs. Yonkers told us, "and kids didn't have computers during the Civil War."

"They didn't?" Ryan said. "How could they get on the internet?"

"There *was* no internet," Mrs. Yonkers said.

"WHAT?!"

"No internet?" I said. "No YouTube?"

Sometimes me and my friends go on YouTube and search for "people falling down" or "hamsters playing the piano."

I could watch
that stuff for hours.

"What a horrible world
it must have been without
computers," Ryan said.

Mrs. Yonkers told us that during
the Civil War there were no calculators,
no DVD players, no iPods, no airplanes, no
cars, no lightbulbs, and no video games.

"Did they have cell phones?" asked Neil

the nude kid.

"Cell phones?" Mrs. Yonkers said. "They didn't even have *regular* phones!"

"How about big-screen TVs?" asked Michael.

"Big-screen TVs?" Mrs. Yonkers said. "They didn't even have *small-screen* TVs!"

"WHAT?!" We were all amazed.

"No TVs?" I said. "Those poor kids! How did they survive?"

"Back in Civil War days," Mrs. Yonkers told us, "kids would actually go outside and play."

"Play? Outside?" Ryan asked. "Why would anybody want to do a crazy thing like that?"

"That reminds me," Mr. Granite suddenly said. "We have to go. It's time for fizz ed."

Fizz ed! Yay!

Fizz ed is my favorite part of the day because we get to play sports and games and run around the gym instead of learn boring stuff. Our fizz ed teacher, Miss Small, is off the wall.

We walked a million hundred miles to the gym. But when we got there, Miss Small wasn't around. And the gym smelled funny.

"What's that weird smell?" I asked.

"I think it's incense," said Andrea.

I never heard of that stuff, but it stinks.

I thought I was gonna throw up.

In the far corner of the gym, there was a guy lying on the floor. We all ran over to see if he was okay. That's when I saw that the guy wasn't really lying on the floor. He was lying on a bed made of nails!

A bed made of nails?!

The guy got up. He was wearing a turban on his head.

"Oh, excuse me," he said in a squeaky voice. "I was just taking a nap."

"On nails?" Neil said. "Doesn't that hurt?"

"Not at all," he said. "It is very comfortable. Studies show that children learn faster when they sleep on a bed of nails."

Those kids are weird. I know what I would learn if I slept on nails. I would learn to get off those dumb nails and go to sleep in a *real* bed.

That's when Mrs. Jafee came into the gym.

"Okeydokey!" she said. "I want to

introduce you guys and gals to Swami Havabanana. He's from India."

"Good day," Swami Havabanana said as he bowed to us. "It is a most beautiful morning in which to be alive, is it not?"

"Where's Miss Small?" we all asked.

"Oh, her?" said Mrs. Jafee. "I fired her,

by golly! Swami Havabanana is our new gym teacher."

"WHAT?!"

"Miss Small just wanted to play sports and silly games," said Mrs. Jafee. "What a waste of time. Studies show that sports and games don't help kids learn. Swami Havabanana has some different ideas. Don'tcha, Swami?"

"Oh, yes," he said, "we are going to learn about yoga."

"YOGA?!"

"You mean we're gonna learn about that little dude in *Star Wars*?" I asked.

"That's Yoda, dumbhead," said Andrea, rolling her eyes.

"I knew that," I lied.

"My dad told me there was a guy named Yoga who played for the Yankees," said Michael.

"That's Yogi, dumbhead," said Ryan.

"Yoga is a way to achieve inner peace and tranquillity by performing specific body positions."

I didn't know what the swami guy was talking about.

"This is the camel pose," he said, getting down on his knees and leaning his head all the way back. "And this is the cobra pose. And this is the fish pose."

Swami Havabanana twisted himself up into a bunch of weird positions.

"Can we do the football pose?" asked Neil the nude kid.

"I never heard of that one," Swami said. "But who wants to try a yoga pose?"

"Me! Me! Me! Me!" shouted Andrea, waving her hand around like she was washing a window.

Andrea volunteers for everything so teachers will like her. If a teacher said they needed a kid to jump off the roof, Andrea would volunteer.

Of course Swami Havabanana picked her.

"I need a boy, too," he said.

Me and the guys looked at our feet so we wouldn't get picked. If you look at your feet, the teacher will never call on you. That's the first rule of being a kid.

The only problem was that Ryan, Michael, and Neil were all fake coughing into their hands and muttering "A.J. . . . A.J. . . . A.J."

"Where is A.J.?" asked Swami Havabanana.

"Over there!" all the guys said, pointing at me. Michael gave me a shove, and Swami told me to stand next to Andrea.

Mrs. Jafee said she had to go check on the other classes.

"I betcha Swami Havabanana will have you guys and gals very relaxed!" she said. "Okeydokey, I'll be back in a jiffy to see how A.J. and Andrea are making out."

"Oooooh!" Ryan said. "A.J. and Andrea are going to be making out! They must be in *love*!"

"When are you gonna get married?" asked Michael.

If those guys weren't my best friends, I would hate them.

I Thought I Was Gonna Die

Swami Havabanana told me and Andrea to stand back-to-back and link our elbows together.

"Ewww, disgusting!" I said. "Her butt is touching my butt."

"Oh, be quiet, Arlo," said Andrea.

"This is called the double chair pose," Swami said. "As you lean against each other, take a few small steps forward."

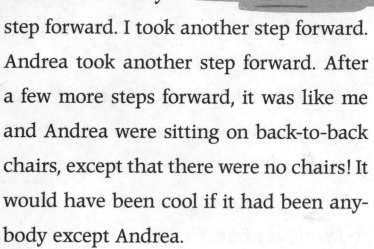

I leaned against Andrea and took a tiny step forward. Andrea took a tiny step forward. I took another step forward. Andrea took another step forward. After a few more steps forward, it was like me and Andrea were sitting on back-to-back chairs, except that there were no chairs! It would have been cool if it had been anybody except Andrea.

"See?" said Swami Havabanana. "They are like matching chairs."

"Oooooh!" Ryan said. "A.J. and Andrea are like matching chairs! They must be in *love*!"

"Yoga means 'to join,'" Swami Havabanana said, as he helped me and Andrea up. "It will take us on a journey of discovery as we go in search of the life force that will awaken every cell and balance our mind, body, and spirit."

"Can we just go play football?" asked Neil the nude kid.

"Football is a game of violence and aggression," the swami said.

"Yeah," I told him. "That's why we want to play it."

Swami told us all to sit on the floor with

our legs crossed. Then we had to take our feet and sort of cross our legs *again*. I thought I was gonna *die*. Now I know what it feels like to be a pretzel.

"Very good!" said Swami Havabanana. "That is called the lotus position."

He taught us a bunch of other positions, like the downward dog, the roaring lion, the flying crow, and the sleeping tortoise.* Swami Havabanana said we could invent our own poses, too.

"Look, I can touch my toes," said Emily.

"I can crack my knuckles," said Michael.

"I can crack my nose," said Neil.

---

* I didn't even know animals did yoga.

"I can make my eyelids turn inside out," I said.

"Yoga is fun, is it not?" Swami asked.

"Yes!" said all the girls.

"No!" said all the boys.

Next, we had to lie on the floor and practice breathing, which made no sense at all because any dumbhead knows how to breathe. Breathing is way overrated.

"Breathe in . . . and breathe out," said Swami Havabanana. "Are you breathing?"

"Yessssssssssssssss . . . ," we all said.

Swami told us that deep breathing calms the nervous system. What's up with that? It's called the *nervous* system.

It's *supposed* to be nervous.

"Let go of the tension in your muscles," he said. "Are you relaxing?"

"Yesssssssssssssss . . ."

"Feel the soothing calmness take over your inner being. . . ."

"Yessssssssssssss . . ."

"Only when the mind is still can the true essence of life be achieved. Find your deepest self. . . ."

"Yesssssssssssssss . . ."

"Feel the flowing life energy."

"Yesssssssssssssss . . ."

"Can you see the universe unfolding in your mind?"

Zzzzzzzzzzzzzzzzzzzzzzzzzzzzzzzzzzzzzzzzzzzz

ZZ

ZZ

ZZZ

ZZZ

ZZZ

ZZZ

ZZZ

ZZZ

ZZZ

ZZZZZZZZZZZZZZZZZZZZZZZZZZZZZZZZZZZZZZZZZ . . .

I was having a dream about Yoda and Yogi doing yoga on YouTube. Then they all started fighting. Yoda had a light saber, and Yogi had a baseball bat. It was a cool dream. But suddenly I heard somebody shouting.

"WAKE UPPPPPPPPPPPPP!"

I opened my eyes. Mrs. Jafee was standing there with her hands on her hips. When ladies put their hands on their hips, it means they're mad. Nobody knows why.

"The children were very much relaxed, as you requested," said Swami Havabanana.

"You put them to sleep!" Mrs. Jafee shouted.

"It is but a fine line between sleeping and waking," said Swami Havabanana.

"It's also a fine line between gettin' hired and fired!" Mrs. Jafee yelled. "Get outta here! You're fired!"

"I must go?" asked Swami Havabanana.

"You betcha!" Mrs. Jafee said. "Beat it! And take your doggone bed of nails with you!"

She chased Swami Havabanana out of the gym.

Mrs. Jafee is daffy!

Stonewall Jackson

Every Tuesday after fizz ed we go see Mrs. Roopy in the media center. It used to be called the "library," but over the summer they changed it to the "media center." Nobody knows why.

When we got there, Mrs. Roopy wasn't around, but a guy with a beard was standing at attention in a gray army uniform. He looked a lot like Mrs. Roopy, except that he only had one arm.

"Mrs. Roopy?" we all asked.

"Roopy? Never heard of her," the army guy said. "General Stonewall Jackson, at your service. I am one of the most important Southern generals of the Civil War."

"You couldn't possibly be Stonewall Jackson," Andrea said. "The Civil War took place a hundred and fifty years ago."

"Yes, don't I look young for my age?" said Stonewall Jackson.

I was almost sure he was really Mrs. Roopy in a Stonewall Jackson costume. Mrs. Roopy is loopy.

"What happened to your arm?" Neil the nude kid asked.

"Sit around me on the floor and I'll tell you," Stonewall Jackson said. "It was May

second, 1863, at the Battle of Chancellorsville. In the fog of war, my own men shot me by accident. The doctors had to remove my arm to save my life."

"WOW," we all said, which is "MOM" upside down.

"Why do they call you Stonewall?" asked Ryan.

"It was at the Battle of Bull Run in 1861," Stonewall whispered. "My Virginia brigade was getting beaten badly. One of my men saw me and said, 'Look, there stands Jackson like a stone wall.' The men were so inspired, they went on to victory. Yep, that's how I got this nickname."

Suddenly, the strangest thing in the

history of the world happened—the lights went out. It was completely dark in the media center. I couldn't see my hand in front of my face.

"What happened?" somebody said.

"Everyone remain calm," said Stonewall Jackson. "The power must have gone out."

"Nope," said a voice from the other end of the media center. "I turned out the doggone lights."

"Who said that?" asked Stonewall Jackson.

"Me," said the voice, "Mrs. Jafee."

"Why did you turn out the lights?" Ryan asked.

"During the Civil War they didn't have electric lights," Mrs. Jafee told us. "So people had to get used to being in the dark. And studies show that children learn better in total darkness. I learned that in graduate school. You're not distracted by anything in the dark. It's easier to focus your attention. Okeydokey, I'll be back in a while to see how you guys and gals are making out in the dark."

"Eww, disgusting!" we all said.

"I'm scared," said Emily, the big crybaby.

"Shhhhh, it's okay," Stonewall Jackson whispered. "Let me tell you another Civil War story. It was during the Battle of Gettysburg. A young woman named Jennie Wade was baking bread in her house when she was hit by a stray bullet. She was the only civilian killed during the Battle of Gettysburg."

"WOW," we all said, which is "MOM" upside down.

"That's so sad!" said Emily, who thinks everything is sad.

That's when an announcement came over the loudspeaker.

"Stonewall Jackson, please report to the office," said Mrs. Patty, the school secretary.

"I'll be right back to finish the story," said Stonewall Jackson. "Please remain calm and be on your best behavior."

As soon as Stonewall Jackson left, I got up and shook my butt at the class. But nobody laughed because it was really dark and they couldn't see me.

"It's spooky in here," said Emily.

Somebody started making scary mouth sounds. I think it was Ryan.

"It would be cool if a zombie came in here right now," I said.

"Arlo, stop trying to scare Emily," said Andrea.

"I am a zombie!" Michael said in a zombie voice. "A killer zombie."

"I'm a robot killer zombie," said Ryan.

"I'm a psycho robot killer zombie," said Neil the nude kid.

"Ow!" said Emily. "A.J. poked me!"

"I did not!" I said. "It must have been one of those zombies."

"Stop pushing!" said Andrea.

After that, I'm not exactly sure what happened. Kids were climbing all over me. It was just a jumble of voices.

"Ow, my head!"

"Get off!"

"Get your foot off my face!"

"I hit my head on the pencil sharpener!"

"I think I saw a ghost!"

"I want my mommy!"

"Where's the light switch?"

"Help! I can't breathe!"

"We're all going to die!"

"We're trapped! There's no way out!"

"Run for your lives!"

Suddenly, the lights went back on. Mrs. Jafee and Stonewall Jackson were standing in the doorway. The whole class was a big pile of bodies all over the floor. I was at the bottom of the pile.

"What's going on in here?" demanded Mrs. Jafee.

You could have heard a pin drop. I looked at Michael. Michael looked at me. Ryan looked at me. Neil looked at me. Andrea looked at me. Everybody was looking at me.

I didn't know what to say. I didn't know what to do. I had to think fast.

"We were . . . acting out the Battle of Gettysburg," I said.

"Hmmmmm," said Mrs. Jafee. "Studies show that students learn best when they are doing what they are learning. Excellent! I'm glad you're getting into the spirit of Civil War Week."

A New Way to Learn

When I woke up on Wednesday morning, my mom told me to put on my bathing suit.

"Do I have the day off from school?" I asked hopefully. "Are we going to the beach?"

"No," my mom said. "I got an email from

Mrs. Jafee that said everybody has to wear a bathing suit today."

That's weird! As I crossed Walnut Street in front of the school, the first person I bumped into was Andrea.

"Do you like my new swimsuit, Arlo?" she asked me. "It has polka dots on it."

"So does your face," I said.

Andrea was going to say something mean to me, but she didn't get the chance. Because as we came around the corner to the side entrance of the school, we saw the strangest thing in the history of the world.

There was a swimming pool in the playground!

"WOW,"
I said, which
is "MOM" upside
down.

Me and Andrea
went running over
to the pool. Mrs. Jafee

was standing there in her bathing suit with some kids.

"Where did you get the swimming pool, Mrs. Jafee?" Andrea asked.

"From Rent-A-Pool," she said. "You can rent anything."

Mrs. Jafee told us to go to our class. She said she would call us down when it was our turn to use the pool.

It felt like a million hundred years until Mrs. Patty finally made the announcement over the loudspeaker. . . .

"Will Mr. Granite's class please report to the playground?"

"Yay!" everybody yelled as we ran out of the classroom. Mr. Granite told us not to run, but we were all so excited to go swimming, it was hard not to. We were all out of breath when we got to the pool.

"Can we go swimming now?" Ryan asked.

"Gee golly, no," said Mrs. Jafee. "I didn't get the pool for swimmin'."

"Why did you get it then?" asked Michael.

"For learnin'!" she said. "Studies show that guys and gals learn better underwater."

"WHAT?!"

Mrs. Jafee gave each of us a pair of goggles and a sheet of paper that was covered with plastic. The page had a bunch of words on it, like "Lincoln," "Union," "Grant," "Lee," and "South."

"What are we supposed to do with this?" asked Neil the nude kid.

"I want you to learn how to spell these Civil War vocabulary words," she said. "Okeydokey, everybody into the pool!"

"Can't we just learn the words out here and then go swimming for fun?" asked Michael.

"No!" said Mrs. Jafee, and she pushed Michael into the pool. "You'll learn better underwater."

"But I can't swim!" yelled Emily.

"You'll learn to swim better underwater, too!" Mrs. Jafee said, pushing Emily into the pool.

Then she ran around pushing the rest of us into the water.

"But this isn't any fun!" yelled Ryan.

"Who says learnin' is supposed to be fun?" Mrs. Jafee yelled. "Now get underwater and start memorizin' those words, doggone it!"

Mrs. Jafee picked up a beach ball and bounced it off Ryan's head. I ducked underwater because I didn't want Mrs. Jafee throwing a beach ball at me.

I sat on the bottom of the pool trying to learn the spelling words. When I couldn't hold my breath anymore, I popped up. Everybody was gasping for breath. Emily looked like she was gonna die.

"Okeydokey!" Mrs. Jafee said, jumping into the pool. "It's time for a spellin' test."

"You didn't say there would be a test!" I complained.

"I'm sayin' it *now*!" she said. "So get underwater! You're first, A.J.!"

Mrs. Jafee picked up a beach ball and threw it at my head. I dived underwater.

I opened my eyes, and there was Mrs. Jafee staring at me from a few inches away.

"How do you spell 'glub'?"* she asked. It was hard to hear her underwater.

"What?" I said.

"Glub do you spell 'Lincoln'?" she asked.

---

* "Glub" is the universal language for speaking underwater.

"*L-I-N-C-O-L-glub,*" I said.

"Correct," said Mrs. Jafee, "and glub do you glub glub?"

"Glub?" I asked.

"I said, 'Glub glub glub glub glub?'"

"Glub glub glub glub?" I guessed.

"Nope, I'm sorry," Mrs. Jafee said. "The correct glub is glub glub GLUB glub."

"That's glub I said!"

"No, you said, 'Glub glub glub glub,'" said Mrs. Jafee.

"But glub glub glub glub is the same as

glub glub GLUB glub," I explained.

"No it's not," she said. "You got one of the glubs wrong."

By that time I ran out of breath and had to come up for air.

That was the weirdest spelling test in the history of the world.

Mrs. Jafee's Evil Plan

After we dried off and changed clothes, it was time for lunch in the vomitorium. Me and the guys sat at one table. Andrea and her girly friends sat at the next table. Mrs. Jafee was walking around with a basket.

"Who wants a hardtack?" she asked.

"A heart attack?" I asked. "Why would anybody want one of them?"

"No, silly!" Mrs. Jafee said. "Hardtack is a kind of cracker that soldiers ate during the Civil War. It's made from flour, salt, and water. I baked this batch myself, you betcha!"

Hardtack sounded disgusting. Ryan said he would try a piece, because he will eat anything, even stuff that isn't food. One time he took a bite out of the seat cushion on the school bus.

Mrs. Jafee gave Ryan a piece of hard-tack.

He bit into it.

"It tastes like cardboard," he said.

Only Ryan would know what cardboard tastes like. Who eats cardboard? Ryan is weird. The rest of us told Mrs. Jafee that we didn't want any hardtack. She said she had to go back to her office.

"I can't wait until Civil War Week is over," Michael said.

"Yeah, and Mr. Klutz will get back from Principal Camp," said Neil the nude kid. "Mrs. Jafee is weird."

"Maybe Mrs. Jafee isn't a real vice principal," I said. "Did you ever think of that?"

"Yeah," Michael said, "maybe she kidnapped our real vice principal and has her trapped in a bamboo cage that's hanging from a tree in the jungle. Stuff like that happens all the time, you know."

"Stop trying to scare Emily," said Andrea at the next table.

Emily looked like she was going to cry. As usual.

"I'll tell you what I think," said Ryan. "Mrs. Jafee is trying to take over Mr. Klutz's job. She didn't send him to Principal Camp so he would be a better principal. She sent him to Principal Camp so she could have him *murdered*!"

"No!" said Emily. "It can't be true!"

"I saw that in a movie once," said Michael. "I'll bet Mrs. Jafee is sitting in her office right now stroking a cat and plotting how to murder Mr. Klutz. Villains always stroke cats while they plot how to murder people."

"We've got to *do* something!" Emily said, and then she went running out of the vomitorium.

And do you know what? For once in her life, Emily was right. We *did* have to do something.

We all scraped off our trays. Instead of going out for recess, we slinked down the hall to the office. We were slinking around like secret agents. It was cool.

Finally, we got to Mrs. Jafee's office. The door was open a crack. We peeked in. And

you'll never believe in a million hundred years what Mrs. Jafee was doing in there.

She was stroking a cat!

"See?" Michael whispered. "I *told* you she's plotting to murder Mr. Klutz!"

"Howdy, guys and gals!" Mrs. Jafee suddenly said. "Come on in! Meet my new kitten. His name is Mister Fur Columbus."

"He's adorable!" Andrea said, running over to pet the cat.

"No, he isn't!" I said. "That cat is evil! And you, Mrs. Jafee, will stop at nothing to turn your evil plan into reality!"

"Huh?" Mrs. Jafee said. "What evil plan?"

"You want to be principal, don't you?" asked Michael.

"Well, someday maybe, yes, I suppose," said Mrs. Jafee.

"Aha!" Ryan said. "So you admit it! You sent Mr. Klutz away to be murdered so you could take over the school!"

"That's silly," Mrs. Jafee said. "I told you. Mr. Klutz is at Principal Camp."

"Liar!" I shouted.

"Here, I'll prove it to you," Mrs. Jafee said, pulling a piece of paper from her desk drawer. This is what it said.

Dear Mrs. Jafee,

I'm having a wonderful time at Principal Camp. This morning we made lanyards. We also had rock climbing, archery, and parachuting. I hope to learn how to swim tomorrow. I never learned when I was a boy. Tell the kids I miss them.

Sincerely,

Mr. Klutz

There was also a photo of Mr. Klutz paddling a canoe.

"See!" I said to Andrea. "I *told* you they have canoes at Principal Camp!"

"Well, I guess you're not planning to murder Mr. Klutz after all," Michael said.

"Of course not!" said Mrs. Jafee.

We all stroked Mister Fur Columbus before we left. But I didn't trust either of them for one minute. I was sure Mrs. Jafee had something up her sleeve.

And not just an arm.*

---

* I mean, everybody has an arm up their sleeve. Except for that Stonewall Jackson guy. He has a sleeve with no arm up it.

The Greatest Moment of My Life

On Thursday morning we were doing math in our class when Mrs. Patty's voice came over the loudspeaker.

"Mr. Granite, please send A.J. to Mrs. Jafee's office."

Bummer in the summer!

"Ooooh!" Ryan said. "You're in trouble, A.J."

"Maybe you'll get kicked out of school for all the mean things you've said to me, Arlo," said Andrea.

"Your face should get kicked out of school," I told her.

I walked down the hall real slowly, just in case I was in trouble. If you ever get called down to the principal's office, walk as slowly as you possibly can. That's the first rule of being a kid.

"Am I in trouble?" I asked when Mrs. Jafee opened her door.

"Heavens no!" Mrs. Jafee said. "Come on in."

And you'll never believe in a million hundred years what she had on her desk.

I'm not gonna tell you.

Okay, okay, I'll tell you.

Mrs. Jafee's desk was filled with cake, cookies, candy, and a tub of ice cream!

"You gave me an idea yesterday, A.J." Mrs. Jafee told me. "You said guys and gals would learn better if they ate ice cream, cookies, cake, and candy. So, dog-gone it, I decided to do an experiment to see if that was true."

"You mean I get to eat all this?" I asked.

"You betcha! Have a seat."

This was even better than the time Mr. Klutz gave me a candy bar! This was the greatest moment of my life.

I sat down, and Mrs. Jafee handed me a book called *Civil War Stories for Kids*. She told me to read the first chapter.

"Can I have a cookie while I read?" I asked.

"You betcha!" Mrs. Jafee said. "That's the whole idea of the experiment. Eat as many cookies as you want."

I took a cookie from the plate and ate it while I read the first page of the book. I hate reading, but it wasn't so bad because I had a cookie.

"Can I have some candy?" I asked when the cookie was done.

"Okeydokey!" Mrs. Jafee said. "Eat up!"

I gobbled down some M&M's, jelly beans, and a KitKat bar while I read from the book. I couldn't wait to tell everybody in class that Mrs. Jafee gave me junk food. They would be so jealous!

"Have a hunk of cake," Mrs. Jafee said.

"Don't mind if I do!" I said.

I kept reading chapter one in the book while I ate. It was about a drummer boy who had to fight in the war.

"How about some ice cream?" Mrs. Jafee asked. "It's Moose Tracks."

"My favorite flavor," I said.

Mrs. Jafee put a big scoop of ice cream in a bowl and gave it me. It was great, but I was starting to get full.

"More candy," Mrs. Jafee said.

"No, thank you," I told her. "I'm going to take a little break."

"I wasn't askin' you if you wanted more candy, A.J.," she said. "I was *tellin'* you that I'm *givin'* you more."

"Oh," I said. "Okay. Can I bring some of it home with me to eat later?"

"Nope, sorry," Mrs. Jafee said. "The experiment must be completed on school grounds."

I took a Twix bar and ate it. My stomach was starting to feel a little funny.

"More cake," said Mrs. Jafee.

"But—"

"I *said*, 'MORE CAKE'!" shouted Mrs. Jafee. She stuck a fork full of the stuff into my mouth like I was a baby.

"More ice cream!" she said, taking a big scoop with a long spoon.

"Do I have to?" I asked with some of the cake dribbling out of my mouth.

"YOU BETCHA!"

I swallowed the ice cream. I was starting to feel sick.

"MORE CANDY!" she said.

"No more!" I begged. "Please! Stop! I'll do anything!"

"EAT IT!" Mrs. Jafee yelled. "You must

eat *all* this junk food to complete the experiment."

I thought I was gonna die.

The Un-Civil War

Well, I know one thing—studies do *not* show that kids learn better if we eat lots of ice cream, cookies, cake, and candy. After the experiment in Mrs. Jafee's office, I had to go home and lie down for the rest of the day. I may never eat junk food again. Or at least, not for a few days.

The next morning was Friday, the best day of the week.* I was a little late getting to school. By the time I arrived, everybody was in the playground. I ran over there and found the kids in my class.

"What's going on?" I asked Ryan.

"Beats me," he replied.

That's when two guys in army uniforms marched out of the gym. One of them was that guy Stonewall Jackson, who I'm pretty sure was really our librarian, Mrs. Roopy. The other one was wearing a blue uniform and a beard. But it was obviously Mrs. Jafee.

"You guys and gals gave me an idea the other day," she said. "Studies show the

_____

* Except for Saturday and Sunday, of course.

90

best way to learn is to *do* the thing you're learning. So I thought the best way to learn about the Civil War would be to reenact it, right here at Ella Mentry School!"

"WHAT?!"

"We're gonna have a war in the playground?" one of the fourth graders asked.

"You betcha!" Mrs. Jafee said. "I will be General Grant of the Union army. And you know General Stonewall Jackson of the Confederate army. Any questions?"

"Are we going to use real guns?" Andrea asked. "Guns are dangerous."

"Of course not," said Mrs. Jafee. "We will act out the war with water guns."

The teachers came out of the gym and

passed out Super Soakers to everybody. It was cool.

Mrs. Jafee told everybody in second and third grade to go to one end of the playground and everybody in first and fourth grade to go to the other end. The kindergarten kids were given drums to play on the side, because they're too little to handle Super Soakers.

Stonewall Jackson led us to our end of the playground. We all gathered around

him, I mean her.

"Kids," she said, "we, the people, have nothing to fear but fear itself. Four score and seven years ago, the torch was passed to a new generation. And now, it's morning in America."

I didn't know what she was talking about.

"Charge!" Mrs. Jafee suddenly yelled from across the play- ground.

I looked up and saw about

a hundred kids screaming as they ran toward us with Super Soakers. I thought I was gonna die!

"Don't fire till you see the whites of their eyes!" Stonewall Jackson shouted.

After that it was all pretty confusing. Kids were running all over the place, screaming and shooting water everywhere. Some of those fourth graders were big kids. They were drenching our second graders. We were all getting soaked. Kids were falling down, freaking out, and calling out for their mothers.

"Run for your lives!" shouted Neil the nude kid.

"Retreat! Retreat!" hollered Stonewall Jackson, and we all gathered around her again at the back of the playground.

"Listen up," she said. "Those Yankees are beating us badly."

"Yankees?" I asked. "Why would we fight a baseball team?"

Everybody laughed even though I didn't say anything funny. Andrea rolled her eyes.

"I thought this was supposed to be a *civil* war," she complained. "It doesn't seem very civil to me."

"What are we gonna do, General Jackson?" asked Michael.

"There's only one thing we *can* do," Stonewall Jackson said. "We need to capture Mrs. Jafee, I mean General Grant."

"WHAT?!"

"It's our only hope," Stonewall said. "I need two volunteers."

Andrea waved her hand in the air, of course, so she got picked. I looked at my shoes so Stonewall wouldn't call on me.

"Andrea," Stonewall said, "I need you and A.J. to go on a very dangerous mission."

"Why me?" I protested.

"Oooooh!" Ryan said. "A.J. and Andrea are going on a dangerous mission together! They must be in LOVE!"

"When are you gonna get married?" asked Michael.

"Shhhhhhh!" Stonewall Jackson said. "I need you two to sneak through the woods in the back of the playground, come up behind enemy lines, and capture Mrs. Jafee."

"How are we gonna do that?" I asked.

"With this," Stonewall said, pulling out a big cloth sack.

"Yes, sir!" Andrea said, taking the sack and saluting.

"Good luck," said Stonewall Jackson. "We're counting on you two. Don't let us down."

Me and Andrea sneaked off into the woods. It was a long walk to the other side of the playground.

"I'm scared, Arlo," Andrea said. "Hold my hand."

"Soldiers don't hold hands," I told her.

"We could get ambushed by the enemy

out here," Andrea said. "Hold my hand, Arlo."

"No!"

"Please, Arlo?"

"I'm not holding your hand, and that's final," I said.

That's when I spotted Mrs. Jafee. She was all by herself, leaning against a tree and taking a drink from a water bottle.

"Look!" I whispered to Andrea. "There she is!"

"Shhhhhh!"

We sneaked up behind the tree. We were just a few feet away from Mrs. Jafee. I could hear her breathing. Andrea lifted the sack in the air and pulled it down over

Mrs. Jafee's head.

"What the—"

But Mrs. Jafee didn't have the chance to finish her sentence. She was in the sack.

Arurahruhmrah

"Quick!" Andrea shouted. "Take her legs, Arlo!"

We picked up the sack with Mrs. Jafee in it and rushed back through the woods.

"Help!" Mrs. Jafee shouted. "Put me down, doggone it! I'm your vice principal!"

"No," I said, "you're a prisoner of war!

And in the words of Abraham Lincoln, 'Nah-nah-nah boo-boo on you.' "

"Arlo, I don't think Abraham Lincoln ever said that," Andrea told me.

"Well, he should have."

Andrea and I finally made it back to our side of the playground. We dumped the sack on the ground in front of Stonewall Jackson.

"Great work!" Stonewall said. "Put a gag in her mouth to keep her quiet. I mean *him*."

Ryan and Michael wrapped a rag around Mrs. Jafee's mouth and tied it in the back.

"What do we do now?" asked Neil the nude kid.

"Tie her up with this rope!" Stonewall Jackson said.

Neil tied up Mrs. Jafee. Everybody started yelling and cheering as word got around that our side had captured General Grant.

"We won!" kids were shouting. "We won the war!"

We were all yelling and screaming and celebrating when the strangest thing in the history of the world happened.

A plane flew overhead.

Well, that wasn't the strange part, because planes fly overhead all the time. The strange part was that something was falling out of the plane.

"What's that?" Emily yelled.

"It's a parachute!" yelled Stonewall Jackson.

"They didn't have parachutes during the Civil War," Andrea said. "They didn't have planes either."

It didn't matter what they had during the Civil War because the parachute was coming down right over our heads.

"It's a man!" Ryan shouted.

"It's a man with no hair!" Michael shouted.

"It's Mr. Klutz!" Neil shouted.

"Hooray for Mr. Klutz!" everybody started shouting. "He's back!"

Everybody was happy to see Mr. Klutz again. But there was just one problem. His parachute was heading straight for the swimming pool at the side of the playground.

SPLASH!

It was a real Kodak moment. We saw it live and in person. Everybody ran over to the swimming pool.

"Help!" Mr. Klutz yelled. "I can't swim! Glub glub glub glub!"

Stonewall Jackson jumped into the pool and fished out Mr. Klutz before he drowned.

"Why didn't you go to the airport?" Ryan asked him.

"Well," Mr. Klutz said, "I saw the school out the window of the plane; and since I learned parachuting at Principal Camp,

I thought that jumping out of the plane would be a lot faster than going to the airport."

Mr. Klutz is nuts.

"We missed you so much!" said Andrea, the big brownnoser.

"I missed you all too," Mr. Klutz said. "Where did this swimming pool come from?"

"Rent-A-Pool," I said. "You can rent any-thing."

"But why is it in the playground?" he asked. "I nearly drowned."

"It was Mrs. Jafee's idea," Ryan said. "She said studies show kids learn better under-water."

"Where *is* Mrs. Jafee?" asked Mr. Klutz.

"She's, uh . . . tied up," I said.

That's when Mrs. Jafee came hopping out of the woods. She was still tied up in the sack. It was hilarious.

"What's the meaning of all this, Mrs. Jafee?" asked Mr. Klutz.

"Arurahruhmrah," said Mrs. Jafee.

Or at least I *think* that's what she said. It was hard to tell because she had a gag in her mouth.

"I thought I told you I wanted everything to be nice and calm while I was away," Mr. Klutz said. "It looks like there's a *war* going on out here."

"Arurahruhmrah," Mrs. Jafee replied.

Well, that was pretty much the end of Civil War Week. Mr. Klutz helped us untie Mrs. Jafee and take the gag out of her mouth. Maybe she'll stop trying to teach us her weird ways to learn. Maybe Mr. Klutz will learn how to swim. Maybe Swami Havabanana will get a job as a fizz ed teacher in India. Maybe Miss Small will get her job back. Maybe Mrs. Jafee will stop saying weird stuff like "You betcha!" and "okeydokey." Maybe I'll get to eat more cake, cookies, ice cream, and candy. Maybe we'll be able to talk Mr. Klutz into going to the airport like a normal person instead of jumping out of planes.

But it won't be easy!

If you thought Mrs. Jafee was weird, wait
till you meet Dr. Brad!

My Weird School Daze #7

Dr. Brad Has Gone Mad!

Little Miss Perfect

My name is A.J. and I hate school.

It was Monday morning. I had just walked into Mr. Granite's third-grade class. Everybody was putting stuff into their cubbies. My friends Ryan and Michael were talking about a football game they had watched over the weekend. Andrea Young, this annoying girl with curly brown hair, was talking with her friend

Emily about jewelry.

"Do you like my new necklace?" Andrea asked Emily. "It says *love* on the back."

"It's really shiny," Emily said, "and it goes so nicely with your skirt."

"I love to accessorize!" Andrea said.

Ugh. Girls are so annoying. I didn't even know what "accessorize" meant, but it was obviously some girly thing that girls do.

"G'day, mates!" said Mr. Granite. "Take out your reading log."

Reading log?

I don't have a reading log. Who wants to read a log? How would you write on a log, anyway? I guess you'd have to carve into it with a knife. But how would I carry a log to school? My backpack is heavy enough without having to put a log in there.

"I don't have a—" I started to say.

"He means your notebook, dumbhead," Andrea whispered to me, rolling her eyes.

"I knew that," I lied.

The Human Homework Machine thinks she is *sooooooo* smart. Me and the guys call her Little Miss Perfect. For fun, Andrea reads the dictionary.

What is her problem? Why can't a reading log fall on her head?

Actually, I didn't have to take out my reading log after all. Because at that moment, the most amazing thing in the history of the world happened. There was a knock on the door.

Well, that's not the amazing part,

because doors get knocked on all the time. The amazing part was what happened next.

"A.J.," Mr. Granite said, "will you please answer the door?"

"How can I answer the door?" I asked. "Doors don't talk."

"*I'll* do it," said Andrea, rolling her eyes again.

Little Miss Perfect opened the door. The school secretary, Mrs. Patty, was standing there.

"Mr. Granite," she said, "will you please send A.J. to Mr. Klutz's office?"

"*Ooooooooooooooooooooooooh!*" everybody ooooohed.

"A.J.'s in *trouble*!" said Michael, who

4

never ties his shoes.

"What did you do *this* time, A.J.?" asked Ryan, who will eat anything, even stuff that isn't food.

"Did you rob a bank?" asked Neil, who we call the nude kid even though he wears clothes.

"Maybe you'll finally get kicked out of school, Arlo," said Andrea, rubbing her hands together.

Andrea calls me by my real name because she knows I don't like it.

"Your *face* should get kicked out of school," I told Andrea.

I thought about all the bad things I had done recently. Maybe it was the time I put a worm in Emily's sneaker during recess.

Maybe it was the time I wrote *kick me* on a piece of paper and taped it to Andrea's back when she wasn't paying attention. I must have done something really horrible to be sent to Mr. Klutz's office.

Bummer in the summer! I wanted to run away to Antarctica and go live with the penguins. Penguins are cool. They never get sent to the principal's office.

I walked really slowly down the hall. The slower you walk, the longer it takes to get anywhere. If you walk slow enough, by the time you get to the principal's office, he might forget the bad thing that you did. So always walk to the principal's office *really* slowly. That's the first rule of being a kid.

Finally, after about a million hundred hours, I reached Mr. Klutz's office.

I put my hand on the doorknob.

I turned the doorknob.

I pulled open the door.

And you'll never believe the amazing thing I saw in there.

I'm not gonna tell you what it was.

Okay, okay, I'll tell you. But you have to read the next chapter first. So nah-nah-nah boo-boo on you!

Check out the My Weird School series!

#1: Miss Daisy Is Crazy!
The first book in the hilarious series stars A.J., a secon grader who hates school—and can't believe his teach hates it too!

#2: Mr. Klutz Is Nuts!
A.J. can't believe his crazy principal wants to climb to t top of the flagpole!

#3: Mrs. Roopy Is Loopy!
The new librarian thinks she's George Washington one d and Little Bo Peep the next!

#4: Ms. Hannah Is Bananas!
The art teacher wears clothes made from pot holders. Wo than that, she's trying to make A.J. be partners with yuc Andrea!

#5: Miss Small Is off the Wall!
The gym teacher is teaching A.J.'s class to juggle scarv balance feathers, and do everything *but* play sports!

#6: Mr. Hynde Is Out of His Mind!
The music teacher plays bongo drums on the principa bald head! But does he have what it takes to be a real ro and-roll star?

#7: Mrs. Cooney Is Loony!
The school nurse is everybody's favorite—but is she hidi a secret identity?

#8: Ms. LaGrange Is Strange!
The new lunch lady talks funny—and why is she writing sec messages in the mashed potatoes?

#9: Miss Lazar Is Bizarre!
What kind of grown-up *likes* cleaning throw-up? Miss La is the weirdest custodian in the world!

#10: Mr. Docker Is off His Rocker!
The science teacher alarms and amuses A.J.'s class with wacky experiments and nutty inventions.

#11: Mrs. Kormel Is Not Normal!
A.J.'s school bus gets a flat tire, then becomes hopelessly lost at the hands of the wacky bus driver.

#12: Ms. Todd Is Odd!
Ms. Todd is subbing, and A.J. and his friends are sure she kidnapped Miss Daisy so she could take over her job.

#13: Mrs. Patty Is Batty!
A little bit of spookiness and a lot of humor add up to the best trick-or-treating adventure ever!

#14: Miss Holly Is Too Jolly!
Mistletoe means kissletoe, the worst tradition in the history of the world!

#15: Mr. Macky Is Wacky!
Mr. Macky expects A.J. and his friends to read stuff about the presidents...and even dress up like them! He's taking Presidents' Day way too far!

#16: Ms. Coco Is Loco!
It's Poetry Month and the whole school is poetry crazy, thanks to Ms. Coco. She talks in rhyme! She thinks boys should have feelings! Is she crazy?

#17: Miss Suki Is Kooky!
Miss Suki is a very famous author who writes about endangered animals. But when her pet raptor gets loose during a school visit, it's the kids who are endangered!

#18: Mrs. Yonkers Is Bonkers!
Mrs. Yonkers builds a robot substitute teacher to take her place for a day!

#19: Dr. Carbles Is Losing His Marbles!
Dr. Carbles, the president of the board of education, is fed up with Mr. Klutz and wants to fire him. Will A.J. and his friends be able to save their principal's job?

#20: Mr. Louie Is Screwy!
When the hippie crossing guard, Mr. Louie, puts a love potion in the water fountain, everyone at Ella Mentry School falls in love!

#21: Ms. Krup Cracks Me Up!
A.J. thinks that nothing can possibly be as boring as a sleepover in the natural history museum. But anything can happen when Ms. Krup is in charge.